# Gobble Gobble

By Cathryn Falwell

Dawn Publications

Library of Congress Cataloging-in-Publication Data
Falwell, Cathryn.
Gobble, gobble / by Cathryn Falwell. -- 1st ed.
p. cm.
Summary: A child observes wild turkeys through the seasons. Includes facts about this classic American bird.
ISBN 978-1-58469-148-8 (hardback) -- ISBN 978-1-58469-149-5 (pbk.)
[1. Stories in rhyme. 2. Turkeys--Fiction.] I. Title.
PZ8.3.F2163Go 2011
[E]--dc22

2011011698

Book design and production by Patty Arnold, *www.menageriedesign.net*
Manufactured by Regent Publishing Services, Hong Kong
Printed June, 2011 in ShenZhen, Guangdong, China
10 9 8 7 6 5 4 3 2 1
First Edition

**Dawn Publications**
**12402 Bitney Springs Road**
**Nevada City, CA 95959**
**530-274-7775**
**nature@dawnpub.com**

For the
Curran Family

Spring is here!

Arrows mark the muddy ground . . .

Striped brown feathers are all around . . .

What's that funny gobbling sound?

Turkeys!

A flock of birds with big strong feet.

Turkeys look for seeds to eat.

One day I wake
and look outside.

Turkey toms
spread feathers
wide.

Toms strut and
puff to look their
best.

Turkey hens make
shallow nests.

Summer days are
filled with sun.
Turkey babies
hatch and run!

On rainy days I
have to dash.
Turkeys dart
through puddles.
Splash!

When my dog,
Max, goes
racing by,
Turkeys lift
their wings
and fly.

Autumn leaves are red and gold.

Turkeys crunch with footsteps bold.

The ground
becomes an icy
sheet.
Turkeys skate on
wobbly feet.

Cold winds blow
and bring a freeze.
Turkeys roost up
in the trees.

Winter brings the
first white snow.
Turkey footprints
make a row.

Feathers fluffed
for winter chills,
Will turkeys slide
down slippery
hills?

The year is
coming to an end.
Turkeys know
that I'm their
friend.

# Jenny's Journal

Hi!

Watching wild turkeys in my backyard is so much fun! I wanted to know more about them, so I went to my public library. Here are some things I found out:

Turkeys raised for food that people eat are called *domestic* turkeys. These turkeys look different than wild turkeys. They are bigger, slower moving, and can't fly.

*Here's my picture of a domestic turkey...*

Long ago, wild turkeys lived in much of North America, especially throughout the east and Midwest. They were an important food source for many Native Americans. When the first Europeans arrived in the New World, there were millions of wild turkeys throughout the land. But over time, these important large birds began to disappear. Towns and farms took over the woods and fields that wild turkeys need to live, and too many turkeys were killed.

In the 1970s a group of people who were worried that turkeys might vanish forever formed the National Wild Turkey Federation. They worked hard to move wild turkeys into safe areas where they could live and raise their young. Now there are LOTS of turkeys—six different kinds—living in every state except Alaska, and in many parts of Canada and Mexico. They are found in woods and fields—and in my backyard. They are even in towns and cities!

Wild turkeys have very sharp eyesight. They have strong and powerful legs with three toes on each foot. The males also have a sharp, curved spur on the back of each leg.

The male turkeys are called *toms* or *gobblers.* Their heads are mostly red, white and light blue. There's a growth on the tom's head that's called the *snood.* Sometimes it hangs down over his beak. The other fleshy bumps on the tom's head and neck, called *caruncles*, can change color from white to bright red. Toms also have long hair-like feathers, called a *beard*, that grow from their chests. When toms are showing off for females, they puff up their chests, spread out their colorful feathers, and call, "gobble, gobble!"

Females, called *hens*, also have snoods and caruncles, but theirs are pretty tiny. Hens are smaller and aren't as colorful as the males. This helps them hide when they are sitting on their nests. Hens usually lay between 8 and 14 eggs, and sit on them

*These are wild turkey feathers.*

*... and here's my wild turkey.*

for about a month. Baby turkeys are called *poults*. A young male is a *jake*, and a young female is a *jenny* – just like my name! Wild turkeys eat seeds, acorns, berries, leaves, corn, and small reptiles like salamanders. They also eat lots of insects, including ticks. My dog, Max, is really happy about that! When night comes, turkeys roost in trees. It's really amazing to see such big birds sitting high up in tree branches! Remember, wild turkeys are not pets. They can fiercely defend their nests. We need to respect them and watch from a distance.

There's even more information about turkeys at your library or on the internet. Have fun!

Your friend, Jenny

*I made these poults by cutting pieces from a brown paper bag!*

## Jenny's Fun Things To Do!

### Make a Nature Journal!

I write down the animals, birds, insects, and plants I see. Sometimes I draw pictures or write poems. When I find out more interesting facts, I write them down in my journal, too.

### Make cut-paper pictures!

The fancy name is *collage*. You can use all kinds of paper. I have a scrap box where I keep mine. It has old wrapping paper, envelopes, and other scraps I find – even tiny ones! Then all you need is scissors and glue!

### Go outside and see what animals you can find!

I love to watch turkeys, of course. But I also like to watch squirrels, deer, bugs and birds. What will YOU find?

# Animal Tracks

*Can you guess these tracks?*
*What kinds of animals leave tracks where you live?*

*Answers:*
*Top row, left to right: wild turkey, deer, songbird, squirrel*
*Bottom row, left to right: child in sand, child in snow, Max!*

**Cathryn Falwell** is the author and illustrator of nearly two dozen picture books for children. She lives on a small Maine pond where she enjoys watching wildlife from her tree house.

For more information, activities and photographs, please visit Ms. Falwell's website: www.cathrynfalwell.com.

## A FEW OTHER NATURE AWARENESS BOOKS FROM DAWN PUBLICATIONS

The BLUES Go Birding series features a unique team of bluebirds who are crazy about REAL birds! Their delightful antics will introduce a new generation to the wonderful sport of birding.

*The BLUES Go Birding Across America*

*The BLUES Go Birding at Wild America's Shores*

*The BLUES Go Extreme Birding*

*In the Trees, Honeybees* – a remarkable inside-the-hive view of a wild colony of honeybees, along with simple rhymes and solid information.

*Eliza and the Dragonfly* – Almost despite herself, Eliza becomes entranced by the "awful" dragonfly nymph, and before long both of them are transformed.

*Around One Log* – Years after a great oak tree tumbled to the ground, a whole community of animals—salamanders, roly-polies, chipmunks, and many more—made it their home. Is the old tree now dead? Or alive?